SADDLEBACK *Classics*

THE
JUNGLE
BOOK

RUDYARD KIPLING

ADAPTED BY

Janice Greene

SADDLEBACK
PUBLISHING · INC.

The Count of Monte Cristo
Gulliver's Travels
The Hound of the Baskervilles
The Jungle Book
The Last of the Mohicans
Oliver Twist
The Prince and the Pauper
The Three Musketeers

Development and Production: Laurel Associates, Inc.
Cover and Interior Art: Black Eagle Productions

SADDLEBACK PUBLISHING, INC.
Three Watson
Irvine, CA 92618-2767

E-Mail: info@sdlback.com
Website: www.sdlback.com

ISBN 1-56254-291-5

Printed in the United States of America
05 04 03 02 01 00   9 8 7 6 5 4 3 2 1

CONTENTS

1 Mowgli's Brothers 5

2 Kaa's Hunting 13

3 How Fear Came 24

4 The Outcast 31

5 "Tiger! Tiger!" 38

6 Letting in the Jungle 46

7 The King's Ankus 54

8 Red Dog 61

9 The Spring Running 70

1 Mowgli's Brothers

It was a very warm evening when Father Wolf woke up from his day's rest. Mother Wolf lay beside him. Her nose was draped across four tumbling, squealing cubs. The moon rose over the mouth of the cave where they all lived.

"Arugh!" said Father Wolf. "It is time to hunt again." He was about to run downhill when a little shadow crossed the entrance of the cave.

A small voice whined, "Good luck go with you, O Chief of the Wolves. And may your children never forget those who are hungry!"

It was the despised jackal, Tabaqui—the one who runs about making mischief and telling tales.

Father Wolf said stiffly, "Enter then, and look for yourself."

Tabaqui found a bone with some meat on it. Licking it merrily, he said, "Shere Khan has moved his hunting grounds. He will hunt here next."

Shere Khan was the tiger who lived near the Wainganga River, 20 miles away.

Father Wolf cried, "He has no *right*! The Law of the Jungle forbids him to move his hunting grounds without fair warning. He will frighten off the game for ten miles around!"

Mother Wolf said quietly, "His mother did not call him Lungri (the Lame One) for nothing. That is why he has only killed men's cattle. The villagers of the Wainganga are angry with him. Now he has come here to make our villagers angry. They will hunt the jungle for him, and we must be ready to run when they burn the grass."

"*Out!*" snapped Father Wolf.

"I go," said Tabaqui. "But listen! You can hear Shere Kahn coming now. I might have saved myself the message."

From the valley below the cave came the angry whine of a tiger. He had caught nothing and did not care if the whole jungle knew it.

Father Wolf said, "The fool! Does he think our deer cannot hear such noise?"

"Hush," said Mother Wolf. "It is not our deer he hunts tonight. It is Man."

"*Man!*" Father Wolf snorted in disgust. "And on

our ground, too! Who does he think he is?"

The Law of the Jungle forbids every beast to eat Man—except when he is showing his children how to kill. The reason is that man-killing brings white men riding on elephants and carrying guns. Along with them, the white men would bring hundreds of brown men with gongs and torches.

They heard the full-throated "Aaarh!" of the tiger's charge, followed by a howl.

Father Wolf frowned. "The fool! He must have jumped at a woodcutter's campfire again. He probably burned his feet."

"Something is coming up the hill," Mother Wolf warned, twitching one ear. "Get ready."

When the bushes rustled near the cave, Father Wolf sprang. But the big wolf stopped his leap in midair. He landed almost where he left the ground.

"Man!" he snapped. "It's a man's cub. Look!"

Right in front of him stood a naked brown baby who could just walk. The child looked up into Father Wolf's face and laughed.

"A *man's* cub?" said Mother Wolf. "Quickly— bring it into the cave."

Father Wolf's jaws closed gently around the child's back. Then he laid the naked baby down

among the squirming cubs.

"How little and smooth he is! How *bold*!" said Mother Wolf softly. The baby was pushing his way between the cubs to get closer to the mother wolf's warm hide.

"Ahai!" cried Mother Wolf. "Look! He is taking his meal with the others. Was there ever a wolf who could boast of a man's cub among her children?"

Suddenly the moonlight was blocked from the cave by Shere Khan's great head and shoulders. Behind him Tabaqui squeaked, "My lord, it went in here!"

"I have come for my game," said Shere Khan.

"Give me the man's cub at once."

The wolves could see that Shere Khan was furious from hunger and the pain of his burned feet. But Father Wolf knew the mouth of the cave was too narrow for him to enter. "The wolves take orders from the head of the pack," he said, "not from a striped cattle-killer. The man-cub is ours—to kill if *we* choose."

"What talk is this of choosing? Must I beg for what already belongs to me? It is I, Shere Khan, who speaks!"

Mother Wolf sprang forward. Her eyes, like two green moons in the darkness, faced the blazing eyes of Shere Khan. She said, "And it is I, Raksha (the Demon), who answers. The cub is *mine*, Lungri—mine to me! He shall not be killed. He shall live to run with the pack and hunt with the pack. Someday, perhaps he shall hunt *you*! Now go back to the jungle, lame cattle-killer! Go!"

Shere Khan backed out of the cave's mouth. "We will see what the pack will say about this! The cub is mine, and to *my* teeth he will come in the end, you thieves!" he shouted.

Panting, Mother Wolf threw herself down among the cubs. "Shere Khan speaks the truth,"

Father Wolf said. "The cub must be shown to the pack. Will you still keep him, Mother?"

"He came naked and alone, yet he was not afraid!" she said. "Yes, I will keep him. Lie still, O Mowgli, for Mowgli the Frog is what I will call you."

"But what will our pack say?" said Father Wolf.

The Law of the Jungle was clear. It said that when a wolf's cubs are old enough to stand, they must be brought before the pack. This ceremony was to show the other wolves that they belonged.

Father Wolf waited until his cubs could run a little. Then, on the night of the pack meeting, he took them, along with Mowgli and Mother Wolf, to the Council Rock. This was a hilltop covered with stones and boulders.

There on his rock lay Akela, the great gray Lone Wolf. He led all the pack by his strength and cunning. Below him sat 40 or more wolves. They ranged from scarred gray veterans who could handle a buck alone to lively black three-year-olds who only *thought* they could.

Akela cried, "Look well, O wolves!" One by one, the wolves pushed their cubs to the center of the ring for the others to look over. When the time came, Father Wolf pushed Mowgli into the ring. The man-cub sat playing with some pebbles that shone in the moonlight.

A roar came up from behind the rocks. Then Shere Khan cried out, "That cub is *mine*! What have wolves to do with a man's cub?"

Akela didn't even twitch his ears. "And what have wolves to do with the orders of others? Look well!" he commanded.

Now the Law of the Jungle says that if there is any dispute over a cub, he must be spoken for by at least two members of the pack. And these must not include his father or mother.

"Who speaks for this cub?" asked Akela.

There was no answer. Mother Wolf got ready for a fight if it came to that.

Then Baloo rose up. Baloo was the only other creature who was allowed at the pack meetings. He was the sleepy brown bear who taught the wolf cubs the Law of the Jungle. Baloo said, "I speak for the man's cub. There is no harm in him. Let him run with the pack. I myself will teach him."

"We need yet another," said Akela.

A black shadow dropped down into the circle. It was Bagheera the Black Panther. Everyone knew Bagheera, and nobody cared to cross his path. He was as cunning as Tabaqui, as bold as the wild buffalo, and as reckless as the wounded elephant. But his voice was as soft as wild honey and his skin was softer than down.

"O Akela," purred Bagheera, "I have no right to be here. But the Law of the Jungle says the life of a cub may be bought at a price. Am I right?"

"Good! Good! It is the Law," cried the young wolves, who were always hungry.

"To Baloo's word I will add one bull, just killed, not half a mile from here." Bagheera went on. "Will you accept the man's cub in trade for this?"

Then a chorus of voices sang out. "What matter? What harm can a naked frog do us? He will die in the winter rains. He will burn in the sun. Let him run with the pack. Where is the bull, Bagheera?"

When the others went off to find the dead bull, only Akela, Bagheera, Baloo, and Mowgli's own family of wolves were left. Shere Khan, too, had roared off into the night. He was very angry that Mowgli had not been handed over to him.

"Roar well," Bagheera muttered to himself, under his whiskers. "The time will come when this naked frog will make you roar another tune—or I know nothing of Man."

Kaa's Hunting

When Mowgli was a bit older, Baloo began teaching him the Law of the Jungle. Usually, young wolves learn only laws for their own pack. But Mowgli, as a man-cub, had to learn a great deal more by heart. He grew very tired of having to say the same thing over and over a hundred times. But as Baloo said to Bagheera one day, "There is nothing in the jungle too little to be killed. The Master Words of the jungle shall protect him with every stranger he meets. I will call Mowgli and he shall say them. Come, Little Brother!"

Mowgli slid down a half-fallen tree trunk. "I come for Bagheera and not for you, fat old Baloo!" he said rudely.

"That is all one to me," said Baloo, though Mowgli's words hurt him. "Tell Bagheera then. Tell him the Master Words I have taught you this day."

Mowgli gave the Master Words—*We be of one*

blood, you and I—to be used with the Hunting-People, the birds, and the snakes. Then he clapped his hands, jumped on Bagheera's back, and made the worst faces he could think of at Baloo.

"Soon I shall have a tribe of my own," Mowgli boasted. "I'll lead them through the trees, and we'll throw branches and dirt on Baloo!"

Whoof! Baloo scooped up Mowgli's wriggling little body. Lying between Baloo's big paws, the boy could see that the bear was very angry. Mowgli glanced over at Bagheera. The panther's eyes were hard as jade.

"Mowgli," said Baloo, "I see you have been talking with the Monkey-People. I have taught you the Law for all people of the jungle *except* the Monkey-People. They have no Law. They have no leaders. They boast and chatter of all the great things they mean to do. Then the fall of a nut makes them forget everything. We have nothing to do with them. We do not drink where they drink; we do not hunt where they hunt; we do not die where they die."

Baloo had hardly spoken when a shower of nuts and twigs fell down through the branches. They could hear the angry crashing of monkeys high in the tree branches above their heads.

"Baloo," said Bagheera, "you might have warned Mowgli against them."

"How was I to guess he would play with such dirt?" Baloo asked. "The Monkey-People! Faugh!"

When it was time for the midday nap, Mowgli lay down to sleep between the panther and the bear. He was very much ashamed of himself. He told himself he would stay away from the Monkey-People from now on.

But the next thing Mowgli knew there were hands pulling on his arms and legs—hard, strong, little hands. Then he felt a swash of branches across his face. Before he saw what was happening, he was staring *down* through the waving trees!

Below him Baloo and Bagheera woke the jungle with their deep cries. That made the Monkey-People howl with triumph. "Bagheera has finally noticed us!" they cried. "Now all the jungle sees how skillful and cunning we are!"

Then began the wild, whooping flight of the Monkey-People through the trees, carrying Mowgli with them as their prisoner.

At first Mowgli was afraid of being dropped. Then he grew angry and began to think about how to send word to Bagheera and Baloo. But the Monkey-People were traveling fast! He was afraid his friends would never be able to find him.

Looking up, he saw Chil the Kite. Chil had seen that the monkeys were carrying something. He had flown down to see whether their load was anything good to eat.

Mowgli quickly called out to the bird, "*We be of one blood, you and I!*"

Hearing the cry, Chil answered, "In whose name, Brother?"

"Mowgli the Frog! Mark my trail!" shouted Mowgli. "Tell Baloo and Bagheera! Mark my trail!"

Meanwhile, Baloo and Bagheera were frantic with rage and grief. Baloo had set off at a clumsy lope, hoping to catch up to the monkeys somehow.

Bagheera roared at him, "That pace would not tire a wounded cow. This is no time for *chasing*! Sit still and think!"

Baloo stopped and said, "Oh, fool that I am! What Hathi the Wild Elephant says is true: *To each his own fear*. Who do the Monkey-People fear? Kaa the Rock Python. Let us go to Kaa."

"What will he do for us? He is not of our tribe," Bagheera growled.

"But he is very old and very cunning," Baloo said. "And above all, he is always hungry."

They found Kaa, all 30 feet of him, stretched out in the afternoon sun.

"Good hunting!" called Baloo.

"Good hunting for us all," Kaa said in reply. "Is there news of good game nearby? I am as empty as a dry well."

"We are hunting now," answered Bagheera.

"Let me come with you," said Kaa. "I am hungry for a young buck or an ape. On my last hunt I missed my kill. My tail was too loose about the tree, and I came near to falling. The noise awoke the Monkey-People, and they insulted me with evil names."

"They will say *anything*!" Bagheera cried scornfully. "They will even say that the great Kaa is afraid of the he-goat's horns."

The swallowing muscles on the side of Kaa's throat rippled and bulged with anger.

"It—it is the Monkey-People we follow now," said Baloo. The words stuck in his throat. He hated to admit to any interest in the monkeys.

"The trouble is," said Bagheera, "those nut-stealers have stolen away our man-cub."

"A man-cub in their hands may come to great harm," said Kaa. "They also called me—yellow fish, was it not?"

"Worm, *earthworm*," said Bagheera.

Kaa said, "We must remind the Monkey-People to speak well of me, their master. Where did they go with the cub?"

"We thought *you* might know," said Bagheera.

"I? *How?*" said Kaa.

Just then, a voice above them cried, "Up, up! Look *up*, Baloo!"

Baloo looked up to see Chil the Kite. The bird said, "I have seen Mowgli among the Monkey-People. They took him to the Cold Lairs!"

"Good hunting to you, Chil!" said Bagheera. "I will remember you in my next kill!"

"It is nothing," Chil said. "The boy said the Master Words. I could have done no less." And with that, the big bird circled up to his roost.

"The Cold Lairs are half a night's journey," said Bagheera, looking at Baloo. "Follow after us, Baloo. We must go on quick-foot, Kaa and I."

*   *   *

The Cold Lairs was a deserted city on a little hill. Long ago a king had built it. Now the walls surrounding it were slowly falling away. Wild vines grew out of the windows of the empty houses.

The monkeys had set Mowgli down on an ancient stone terrace. By the hundreds they gathered around him. One of the monkeys made a speech. He said that Mowgli's capture marked a new chapter in the history of the Monkey-People. Now they could make Mowgli show them how to weave sticks and canes together as protection from the cold. Mowgli picked up some vines and began to work them in and out. But in a few minutes, the monkeys lost interest and began to pull each other's tails.

Meanwhile, Bagheera and Kaa had arrived at the Cold Lairs. As the big snake made his way slowly over the west wall, Bagheera entered the terrace without a sound. He quickly began striking right and left among the monkeys, causing howls of rage and fright. Suddenly a monkey shouted, "There is only one here! *Kill him! Kill!*"

A mass of biting monkeys closed over Bagheera. Five or six monkeys grabbed Mowgli. They dragged him up the wall of a stone house and pushed him through a hole in the roof. Mowgli fell a good 15 feet. But he fell as Baloo had taught him, and easily landed on his feet unharmed.

Mowgli could hear the furious yells and chattering of the monkeys around Bagheera. He heard Bagheera's deep, hoarse cough as he twisted and bucked under the heaps of monkeys. For the first time since he was born, Bagheera was fighting for his life.

Mowgli called, "To the water tank, Bagheera! Get to the water!"

Bagheera heard the call. Knowing Mowgli was safe, he felt new courage. Slowly, he inched his way to the water tank.

Then, from the ruined wall closest to the jungle, came the deep war-shout of Baloo. He began to bat at the monkeys with his heavy paws. Then Baloo heard a crash and a splash. This told him that Bagheera had fought his way to the water tank, where the monkeys could not follow.

Lifting his dripping chin, Bagheera called to the snake for protection: *We are of one blood, you and I.* Baloo could not help chuckling as he heard the black panther call for help.

Then suddenly, the monkeys scattered, crying "Kaa! It is *Kaa*! Run! Run!"

The Monkey-People feared no one as they

feared Kaa. He could slip along the branches as quietly as moss grows. He could steal away the strongest monkey who ever lived.

Kaa opened his mouth and hissed. The terrified monkeys huddled together, trembling. The Cold Lairs were silent.

"Where is the man-cub?" demanded Kaa.

"Here!" Mowgli called out from the stone house.

Kaa studied the wall of the house until he found a weak spot. Then, nose-first, he gave it half a dozen full-power, smashing blows. When the wall finally fell away in a cloud of dust and rubbish, Mowgli leaped clear. He flung himself between Bagheera and Baloo.

"Oh, no, they have hurt you, my brothers!" cried Mowgli. "You bleed."

Bagheera said, "It is to Kaa we owe the battle."

Mowgli turned to the great python. "I take my life from you tonight," he said solemnly. "My kill shall be your kill if ever you are hungry, O Kaa."

"All thanks, Little Brother," said Kaa. "But now go—for what must follow you should not see."

Kaa glided to the center of the terrace and began to dance. He moved in a big circle, weaving his head from right to left. Then his body made

loops and figures of eight. His coils formed soft, oozy triangles that melted into squares and mounds. He never rested, never hurried, never stopped his low, humming song. It grew darker and darker, until Kaa's coiled body disappeared.

At last Kaa said, "Monkey-People, come forward now—step nearer to me."

The lines of monkeys moved ahead helplessly. Baloo and Bagheera took one step forward, too.

"*Nearer,*" hissed Kaa, and they all moved again.

Mowgli put his hands on Baloo and Bagheera. His touch seemed to startle them—as though they had been awakened from a dream.

Mowgli led his friends away. Yet he still did not understand the power of the great snake. "It is only Kaa making circles in the dust," he said, "and his nose was all sore. Ho! Ho!"

"Mowgli," Bagheera scolded, "his nose was sore on *your* account. Baloo and I are badly bitten on your account. All of this, foolish little man-cub, came of your playing with the Monkey-People."

"True, it is true," said Mowgli, feeling sorrowful and ashamed now. "I am an evil man-cub, and my stomach is sad in me."

"You will learn," said Bagheera. "Now jump on my back, Little Brother, and we will go home."

Mowgli laid his head down on Bagheera's neck and slept.

# 3

How Fear Came

One winter, it hardly rained at all. The spring blossoms were heat-killed before they were born. Then, inch by inch, the heat crept into the heart of the jungle, turning it yellow, brown, and at last black. The pools in the jungle dried up. Food was so scarce that the animals were no more than skin and bone. Bagheera could kill three times in a night and hardly get a full meal. But the want of water was even worse. Although the Jungle-People seldom drink, they drink deeply.

One day Hathi the Wild Elephant saw that only the main channel of the Wainganga carried a trickle of water. That day, he lifted his trunk and called the Water Truce.

By the Law of the Jungle, no animal could kill at drinking places during the Water Truce. So now they all came, starved and worn out—tiger, bear, buffalo, and pig—to drink together.

One furnace-hot evening, Bagheera and Mowgli came to the river. Bagheera looked at the deer and the pig and the buffalo gathered at the water's edge. He said in wonder, "But for the Law, this would be very good hunting."

The deer heard him. A frightened whisper quickly carried along the riverbank, "The Truce! Remember the Truce!"

"*Peace* there!" gurgled Hathi. "This is no time to talk of hunting."

"And who should know that better than I?" Bagheera answered, rolling his yellow eyes. "I am now an eater of turtles, a fisher of frogs."

Then Shere Khan came limping down to the water. He waited a little before drinking, enjoying the nervous glances of the deer.

"*Faugh*, Shere Khan! What new shame have you brought here?" Bagheera asked.

The lame tiger had dipped his chin in the water. Dark oily streaks were floating from it downstream.

"Man!" said Shere Khan coolly. "It is true. I killed an hour ago."

A whisper went up among the animals. "Man! Man! He has killed *Man*!"

"Man!" Bagheera roared out scornfully. "Why?

Was there no other game to be found?"

"I killed for choice, not for food," said Shere Khan with a boastful smirk.

The horrified whisper began again. Hathi spoke quietly. "Your kill was from *choice*?" he asked. When Hathi asks a question, it is best to answer.

"It was my right and my night. You know this, O Hathi," said Shere Khan. His voice was now almost courteous.

"Yes, I know," said Hathi. "Now, since you have drunk your fill, go!"

Shere Khan slunk away. When last comes to last, Hathi is master of the jungle.

Mowgli waited for a minute to pick up his courage. Then he cried, "*What* is Shere Khan's right, O Hathi?"

"It is an old tale," said Hathi. "Keep silence along the riverbank, and I will tell it to you.

"In the beginning of the jungle," Hathi began, "we walked together. We had no fear of one another. In those days, we ate nothing at all except grass and fruit and bark.

"The Lord of the Jungle was Tha, the First of the Elephants. He made the jungle out of deep waters with his trunk. Where he struck with his foot, there rose ponds of good water. He was very busy making new jungles. But he could not walk *everywhere*. That's why Tha made the First of the Tigers the judge of the jungle. He could settle any disputes between the Jungle-People.

"In those days, the First of the Tigers ate fruit and grass along with all the others. He was as large as I am, and yellow all over, with no stripes. The Jungle-People came before him without fear, and his word was Law.

"Yet one night, there was a dispute between two bucks. When the two were arguing before the First of the Tigers, one buck pushed the other with his horns. The First of the Tigers leaped upon the buck and broke his neck. Before that night, none of us had ever killed another.

"Tha soon heard that one of the Jungle-People had been killed. He ordered the trees and the vines of the jungle to mark the killer, so that all might know his shame.

"Then Tha called us all together. 'One of you has brought Death into the jungle,' he said. 'From now on you shall know Fear, and you shall know that he is your master.'

"The Jungle-People said, 'What is *Fear?*'

"'Look till you find,' Tha answered.

"It was the buffaloes who first found Fear. They told the Jungle-People that Fear sat in a cave. They said he walked upon his hind legs and was hairless. So we of the jungle followed the buffalo to the cave. When Fear saw us, he cried out. His very voice filled us with fear—and we ran away.

"From that night on, the Jungle-People did not lie down together. Instead, each tribe kept off to itself—the pig with the pig, the deer with the deer. Horn to horn and hoof to hoof.

"Only the First of the Tigers was not with us. He was hiding, ashamed of what he had done. When he heard of the thing in the cave, he said, 'I will go to this thing and break his neck.' So he ran that night to the cave. The trees and vines marked him as he ran. Wherever they touched him, a stripe was marked on his yellow hide. As you see, his children wear those stripes to this day.

"When the First of the Tigers came to the cave, Fear put out his hand and called him 'The Striped One.' The First of the Tigers ran away, howling.

"So loud did he howl that Tha heard him. 'What is this sadness?' he asked.

"The First of the Tigers said, 'Give me back my

power, O Tha. I am shamed before all the jungle. I have run away from the Hairless One, who called me a shameful name. What have I done, that these stripes are upon me?'

"Tha answered, 'You have killed the buck, and let loose Death in the jungle. With Death has come fear. Now the Jungle-People are afraid of one another—just as you are afraid of the Hairless One.'

"The First of the Tigers beat his head upon the ground. His pride was broken. 'Remember I was once master of the jungle, O Tha. Let my children remember that I was once without shame or fear!'

"Tha said, 'This much I will do. One night a year, if you meet the Hairless One—and his name is Man—you shall not be afraid of him. *He* shall be afraid of *you*. Show him mercy on that night of his fear, for now you know how terrible Fear is.'

"As the year went by, the First of the Tigers remembered that the Hairless One had called him the Striped One, and he was angry. On a certain night, he went to the cave of the Hairless One. There, everything happened just as Tha promised. The Hairless One fell on the ground before him. Then, without hesitation, the First of the Tigers broke his back with one mighty blow.

"When Tha saw what the First of the Tigers had done, he said, 'Is *this* your mercy?'

"The First of the Tigers licked his lips and boldly answered, 'What matter? Look! I have killed Fear.'

"Tha said, 'O blind and foolish! You have untied the feet of Death! *You have taught Man to kill!*'

"That's how it came about that the First of the Tigers taught the Hairless One to kill. All of you know what harm Man has done to the Jungle-People from that day on."

Bagheera turned to Hathi and said, "Do *men* know this—tale?"

Hathi said, "None have known it except the tigers and the elephants. Now you by the river have heard it, and I have spoken." The old elephant then turned away and dipped his trunk in the water. The tale was over.

The Outcast

By the time Mowgli was 10 or 11, Father Wolf had taught him a great deal about the jungle. Every rustle in the grass meant as much to Mowgli as the work of an office means to a businessman.

When the pack met, Mowgli took his place at the Council Rock, too. It was there he discovered his power. If he stared hard at any wolf, the wolf would be forced to drop his eyes. At other times Mowgli would pick long thorns from the paws of his friends, and pluck burrs from their coats.

Shere Khan was always crossing Mowgli's path. Now that Akela was getting old and weak, the tiger had become great friends with the younger wolves of the pack. Shere Khan would call them fine young hunters. Then he would ask them why they let themselves be led by old Akela and a man's cub. "They tell me," Shere Khan would say, "that you dare not look Mowgli in the eyes." Sensing insult, the proud young wolves would growl and bristle.

Bagheera warned Mowgli of Shere Khan's plans. "Shere Khan dares not kill you while Akela leads the pack," he said. "But Akela is old. Soon the day will come when he cannot kill his buck. Then, alas, he will be leader no more. At that time, the pack will turn against him—and against *you*. Shere Khan has been teaching them that a man-cub has no place in the pack."

Mowgli did not understand. "But a man should run with his brothers," he said.

Bagheera said, "Feel under my jaw."

Mowgli did not understand. But he reached up his strong little hand. Under Bagheera's silky chin he could feel a small bald spot.

"No one in the jungle knows I carry that mark," Bagheera said. "It is the mark of a collar. Who would ever guess that I was born among men, in the cages of the king's palace at Oodeypore? That is why I paid the price for you at the Council Rock. I lived in a cage until the night it came to me that I was Bagheera—the panther. *I was not meant to be a man's plaything.* So I broke the silly lock and came away. But I lived among men and I know their ways. In the end, Mowgli, you must go back to men—if the wolf pack does not kill you first, that is."

"But why—why should any wish to kill *me*?" Mowgli asked in confusion.

"Because their eyes cannot meet yours," Bagheera said. "Because you have pulled thorns from their feet. Because you are a *man*. I have it! Go down to the men's huts in the valley. Take some of the Red Flower. Then, when the time comes, you will have a stronger friend than any in the jungle."

By *red flower*, Bagheera meant fire. Every beast lives in great fear of it. No one in the jungle will call it by its proper name.

Mowgli ran down to the bottom of the valley. He stopped suddenly when he heard the yelps of the pack on the hunt and the whimper of the buck they chased. Then the young wolves howled, "*Akela!* Let Akela show his strength!"

Akela must have sprung and missed, for the next sound Mowgli heard was a weak and pitiful yelp as Akela was being knocked over by the buck.

Mowgli did not wait to hear more, but ran on. The cries of the pack grew faint as he ran across the fields where the villagers lived.

Mowgli hid behind the window of a village hut. He said to himself, "Tomorrow is the day of reckoning for both Akela and me."

Through the window, he watched the fire on the hearth. Later that night, he saw a woman get up and feed it black lumps. When morning came, a boy came out carrying a small pot filled with hot charcoal. Mowgli met the boy, snatched the pot from his hand, and disappeared into the mist. The startled boy howled with fear.

All that day, Mowgli fed his fire pot with dry branches. He was laughing that night as he went to the Council Rock.

Akela lay by the side of his rock, a sign that the leadership was open. Bagheera lay close to Mowgli. The fire pot was between the boy's knees. When all the wolves had finally gathered, Shere Khan began to speak.

Mowgli sprang to his feet. "Why do we allow Shere Khan to speak? What does he have to do with the pack?"

Shere Khan roared, "I am sick of this man's cub! Give him to me—or I will hunt here always and not give you one bone!"

Akela raised his old head and said, "Mowgli is our brother in all but blood. He has eaten our food. He has driven game for us. And he has not broken

one word of the Law of the Jungle."

"But he is a man—a *man!*" snarled many in the pack. Most of the young wolves had now begun to gather around Shere Khan.

Mowgli stood up, furious with rage and sadness. "Listen, you!" he cried. "I would have been a wolf with you to my life's end. But now you tell me that I am a man. So I do not call you brothers anymore. No, I call you *dogs*—as a man should. And you will do as I tell you!"

Mowgli threw the fire pot upon the ground. The pack drew back in terror from the leaping flames.

Then Mowgli pushed a dead branch into the fire until the twigs sparkled and crackled.

"I go from you now," Mowgli said. "But first there is a debt to pay." He caught Shere Khan by the fur of his chin. "Stir a whisker, Lungri, and I will ram the red flower down your throat!" Then he struck out at Shere Khan with the burning branch, and the tiger whined in terror.

"*Pah!*" said Mowgli. "Now go! When I come next to the Council Rock, I will bring your hide! All of you—*go!*"

As Mowgli struck out right and left, the wolves ran howling. At last there remained only Akela, Bagheera, and perhaps 10 wolves who had taken Mowgli's part. Then something strange happened. At that moment a great pain began to hurt Mowgli inside. He caught his breath and sobbed.

"What is it? What is happening to me?" he cried out. "Am I dying, Bagheera?"

"No," Bagheera answered. "It is only tears such as men use. Let them fall."

For a long time Mowgli cried as if his heart would break. Then he went to the cave where Mother and Father Wolf waited for him.

"You will not forget me?" Mowgli asked sadly.

"Never while we can follow a trail," said the four cubs. "Come to the edge of the jungle when you become a man. There we will talk to you."

"I will surely come," promised Mowgli. "Tell my friends in the jungle never to forget me!"

The dawn was beginning to break when Mowgli went down to the village alone. It was time to meet those mysterious things called *men*.

5 "Tiger! Tiger!"

After leaving the jungle, Mowgli came upon a great plain where cattle and buffalo were grazing. At one end of the plain was a little village. Mowgli stood at the gate. As he waited there, a crowd of people gathered around him. They pointed and stared at the naked boy.

"They have no manners, these Men-Folk," Mowgli said to himself.

The village priest said to the crowd, "There is nothing to be afraid of. Look at the scars of little wolf bites on him. He is but a wolf-child run away from the jungle."

One of the women cried, "Look closely, Messua! By my honor, the boy is much like your son who was stolen away by the tiger."

The priest was a clever man. He knew that Messua's husband was the richest man in the village. "What the jungle has taken, the jungle has

38

brought back to you," he said. "Take the boy into your house, Messua. And do not forget to honor the priest, for he sees far into the lives of men."

Messua took Mowgli into her hut. There she gave him some bread and a long drink of milk. She looked deep into his eyes. "Nathoo! Nathoo! Do you remember when I gave you new shoes?" She touched his foot. It was almost as hard as horn. "No," she said sadly. "Those feet have never worn shoes. But you are very like Nathoo—and now you shall be my son."

Mowgli thought, "I must soon learn to speak as they do." As Messua talked throughout the day, he imitated her words. Before dark, he knew the names of many things in the hut.

But that night, he would not get in the bed. To him, it looked like a trap. He went outside to sleep. Just before he closed his eyes, a soft gray nose poked him. It was Gray Brother, the oldest of Mother Wolf's cubs.

"Wake," said Gray Brother. "I bring news. Shere Khan's coat was badly burned with the red flower. He has gone away until it grows back. But I must warn you. When he returns, he swears that he will lay your bones in the Wainganga River!"

"I, too, have made a promise," Mowgli replied. "When he comes back, wait for me under the dhak-tree in the middle of the plain. We do not need to walk into Shere Khan's mouth."

"I will wait for you," Gray Brother promised. "You will not forget you are a wolf, then? Men will not make you forget?"

"Never!" Mowgli promised. "But I will always remember that I was cast out of the pack."

"You may be cast out of *another* pack," Gray Brother warned him. "Men are only men, after all— and their talk is like the talk of frogs in a pond."

For the next three months, Mowgli learned the ways of men. He had to wear a cloth around him, which annoyed him horribly. And there were many things he did not understand in the least. The village priest told Mowgli that the god in the temple would be angry if he ate the priest's mangos. So Mowgli picked up the image of the god and brought it to the priest's house. When he said he would be happy to fight the god, there was an awful scandal. Messua's husband had to pay much good silver to comfort the offended god.

Mowgli knew nothing of the castes which separate men. When the potter's donkey fell into a pit, Mowgli pulled it out by the tail. This shocked the villagers, for the potter is a low-caste man, and his donkey, of course, even lower.

At night Mowgli sat with the men under the great fig tree and listened to the tales of Buldeo, the village hunter. Buldeo told stories of gods and men and ghosts. One night Buldeo spoke of the tiger who had carried off Messua's son. It was a ghost-tiger, he said, inhabited by the spirit of a wicked old moneylender. The old man had a limp, the same as the tiger.

"These tales are nothing but cobwebs and moon-talk," Mowgli snorted. "That tiger probably had a limp because he was born lame."

"Oho! It is the jungle brat, is it?" said Buldeo. "If you are so wise, why don't you bring the tiger's hide to Khanhiwara? The government has set a hundred rupees on his life."

The head man of the village said, "It is high time the boy was set to work. Perhaps herding buffalo will teach him some respect for his elders."

Nothing could have pleased Mowgli more. Every morning he set off with other village boys to herd the cattle and buffalo. He rode on the back of Rama, the great herd bull. From the start he made it clear to the other children that he was master.

At last the day came when Mowgli saw Gray Brother sitting under the dhak-tree. "Shere Khan's plan is to wait for you at the village gate this evening," Gray Brother warned. "He is hiding now in the dry ravine of the Wainganga."

"Has he eaten today?" asked Mowgli.

"He killed a pig at dawn, and he has drunk, too," said Gray Brother. "He could never fast—even for the sake of revenge!"

"Oh, fool, *fool*!" said Mowgli. "He plans to wait until he has slept. I know! I could take the herd to the head of the ravine and then sweep down. But someone must block the other end. Can you cut the herd in two for me?"

Gray Brother said, "Not I alone—but I have brought a wise helper."

Akela trotted out from behind a rock.

"*Akela!*" cried Mowgli, clapping his hands. "I might have known you would not forget me. We have big work at hand. Cut the herd in two, Akela. Keep the cows and calves together, and leave the buffaloes alone."

The two wolves ran in and out of the herd. The animals snorted and threw up their heads. At last they separated into two clumps. The other herd-children, watching from half a mile away, ran to the village as fast as their legs could carry them.

Mowgli slipped onto Rama's back. "Drive the bulls away to the left, Akela. And you, Gray Brother—hold the cows together and then drive them into the foot of the ravine."

Mowgli and Akela drove the buffaloes to the top of the ravine. Then Akela gave a full hunting yell and the buffaloes charged down the steep slope.

Shere Khan heard the thunder of their hooves. He ran around the ravine, looking for some way to escape. But the sides of the deep gorge were steep, and he was heavy with food and drink.

Mowgli, riding on Rama's back, saw Shere Khan turn in his direction. Then Rama tripped and stumbled over something soft. The bulls behind him crashed full into the other herd.

Now the cattle were stamping and snorting. Mowgli cried, "Quick, Akela! Break them up. Softly now, softly, Rama! It is all over."

Shere Khan was dead. Mowgli sat down and began to skin the tiger. "His hide will look well on the Council Rock," he said.

Suddenly, Buldeo appeared, and the wolves

quickly dropped out of sight.

"What is this?" said Buldeo. "Why, it is the Lame Tiger! Well, boy, we will overlook your letting the herd run off. Perhaps I will even give you one of the rupees as a reward when I take the skin to Khanhiwara."

"I need the skin for my own use," said Mowgli. "Come, Akela, this man is bothering me."

In the blink of an eye, Buldeo found himself down in the grass, with a wolf standing over him. After a while Mowgli let him go, and the hunter hobbled away to the village as fast as he could.

When Mowgli returned at twilight with the buffaloes, it seemed that half the village was waiting for him at the gate. "It is because I have killed Shere Khan," he said to himself.

But then a shower of stones whistled about his ears. "Jungle demon! Wolf's brat! Go away!" shouted the villagers.

"*Again?*" Mowgli cried in disbelief. "The last time I was sent away it was because I was a man. This time it is because I am a wolf!"

Messua ran up to Mowgli. "Oh, my son! They say you are a demon! I do not believe such a thing, but go now—or they will kill you!"

"Farewell, Messua," Mowgli cried. "I have at least paid for your son's life. Farewell!"

Akela yelled, and the buffaloes charged through the gate, scattering the crowd left and right.

Later that morning, Mowgli laid Shere Khan's hide on the Council Rock. Akela wailed the old call to the wolf pack. Since the fight with Mowgli, the wolves had been without a leader. Now, when the pack had gathered at the Council Rock, they cried, "Lead us again, O Akela! You lead us too, O man-cub."

"No," said Bagheera, who had heard the call and come to the Rock. "You fought for freedom, and it is yours. Eat it, O wolves."

"Both man pack and wolf pack have cast me out," Mowgli said sadly. "Now I must hunt alone in the jungle."

"Not alone," said the four cubs. "We will hunt with you."

6 Letting in the Jungle

For a few days after Mowgli laid Shere Khan's hide on the Council Rock, he stayed with Mother and Father Wolf and the four cubs at their cave. It was there one morning that Akela told him about a man with a gun who was following his trail.

Mowgli was angry. "Men have cast me out! What more do they need?"

The four cubs got ready to follow the man's scent. "We will roll his skull before noon!" promised Gray Brother.

"No!" Mowgli cried out to his wolf brothers. "Man does not eat man!"

"*No?* Were you not a wolf only a moment ago?" Akela asked.

Mowgli was furious. "Must I give reason for all I choose to do?" he snapped.

"Ah! There speaks a man!" muttered Bagheera. "We know that man is the wisest of all. But, sadly, he is also the most foolish." Raising his voice, he added, "Let us see what *this* man means to do."

The man was Buldeo. Mowgli and the wolves and Bagheera watched Buldeo as he puzzled over the trail. Soon, several farmers came along and stopped to talk to the famous hunter.

Buldeo told them he was tracking Mowgli the Devil-Child—a boy who could change himself into a wolf! He said that the people of the village had imprisoned Messua and her husband. They were the parents of the devil-child, after all. Soon they would be burned to death.

Sadly, Mowgli turned to the wolves and Bagheera. "I must look into this," he said. "The man pack will do nothing until Buldeo returns to the village. Sing to them, my brothers. Hold them here until dark!"

The wolves began to sing. The song rumbled, rose, and fell, until it died in a sort of whine. Very soon they heard the men climbing up into the branches of the trees. Buldeo began muttering charms to fend off evil spirits.

Meanwhile, Mowgli ran quickly to the village. He looked into the window of Messua's hut. Sure enough, she and her husband were bound and gagged. The door was shut fast, and four people were sitting with their backs to it.

When Mowgli climbed into the window and cut the ropes, Messua caught him to her heart. "I knew—I knew you would come," Messua sobbed.

Mowgli gritted his teeth as he saw her wounds, for she had been beaten and stoned all morning. "*Who did this?*" he hissed. "There is a price to pay."

Messua's husband said, "All the villagers did. They were jealous because I was too rich. Now they are saying that we are witches—because we called you our son."

Mowgli heard shouting from outside the hut. He knew that Buldeo had returned.

Mowgli pointed to the window. "There lies the road through the jungle. You two go now!"

"But we know nothing of the jungle, my son!" Messua cried out in fear.

Her husband added, "If we could reach Khanhiwara, we may find the English—"

"And what pack are they?" said Mowgli.

"It is said that they govern all the land," Messua explained. "They will not let people burn or beat each other without witnesses. If we can get there tonight, we will live."

"Go to Khanhiwara, then," Mowgli said. "Not a tooth in the jungle will be bared against you. There will be a watch about you."

Messua flung herself at Mowgli's neck and held him. Her husband said, "If we reach Khanhiwara, I will get the ear of the English. Then I will bring such a lawsuit that will eat this village to the bone! I will have great justice."

Mowgli said, "I do not know what justice is— but if you come back at the next rains, you will see what is left here."

Messua and her husband hurried off into the jungle. Just then Bagheera appeared in the hut.

"Soon, the villagers will come to put the woman and her man into the Red Flower," Mowgli told him. "But look, Bagheera—they have disappeared!"

Bagheera said, "*Pah!* This place stinks of Man. But look—here is a bed like the one I lay on in the king's cages of Oodeypore."

The great panther lay down on a cot, cracking it beneath his weight. "Come and sit beside me, Little Brother," he said.

"No," said Mowgli. "The man pack must not know I was part of this."

"Be it so," Bagheera replied. Then the man-cub

and the panther heard the villagers yelling. They were rushing up the street, waving clubs and knives. In a moment, the crowd tore open the door of the hut and stormed inside.

When the light of their torches shone in the room, they saw the great panther lying on the bed. There was a moment of awful silence. The people in the front of the crowd began to claw and tear their way back to the door. Bagheera yawned. The next minute the street was empty.

Bagheera leaped out the window where Mowgli was waiting. "They will not stir again until daylight comes," he said. "And now?"

"I wish to see Hathi," said Mowgli. "Have him come here with his three sons."

"But Little Brother," Bagheera explained, "remember that Hathi is master of the jungle. One does not say, 'come' and 'go' to him!"

"Tell him to come because of what happened on the fields of Bhurtpore," Mowgli said firmly.

Bagheera was not gone long. When he returned, Hathi and his three sons were right behind him.

Mowgli said, "I will tell you a tale of an elephant. It was told to me by a hunter, Buldeo—who sometimes speaks the truth. One day this elephant fell into a trap. A stake in the pit scarred him from above his heel to the shoulder."

Hathi quickly wheeled around and showed his long, white scar.

Mowgli went on, "Men came to take him from the trap, but he broke loose, for he was strong. When his wound was healed, he came back to the fields of these hunters, to the fields of Bhurtpore. There was never a harvest in those villages again.

"You know the village that cast me out? They would throw their own breed into the Red Flower. I hate them!"

"But *I* have no quarrel with them," said Hathi.

"But Hathi, are *you* the only eaters of grass in the jungle?" said Mowgli. "Drive in the deer and the pig. Let in the jungle, Hathi!"

Hathi thought about it. "Do you promise there will be no killing? My tusks were red at the fields of Bhurtpore. I would not wake that smell again."

"Nor I," said Mowgli. "I have smelled the blood of the woman who gave me food. I tell you, Hathi— only the smell of new grass on their doorsteps can take away that smell."

"Now I see," Hathi said. "Yes, Mowgli—your war shall be our war. We will let in the jungle."

Soon a rumor went through the jungle that there was good food and water in the valley. The pigs came first, then the deer and foxes and wild buffalo. They formed a circle around the village, the Eaters of Flesh driving them forward.

Later that night Hathi and his sons stamped through the village fields. They were quickly followed by the deer and pigs. When the villagers looked out the next morning, their crops were lost. And when the village herds were sent out, they found the grazing grounds smooth and bare. Soon they wandered off and joined the wild buffalo.

The villagers tried to hang on, eating what little food was left. They sent men out to gather nuts in the jungle, but the nut gatherers were always watched by shadows with glaring eyes. Soon the men scurried back, afraid, to the safety of the village walls.

Finally, there was nothing to do but leave. As the last family walked out the village gate, they heard the crash of falling house beams. Hathi and his sons were running down the empty streets, kicking and tearing and trampling. One by one the walls crumbled under their feet and turned to yellow mud in the pouring rain.

A month later, the village was nothing but a dirt mound, covered by shoots of young green grass. By the end of the rains, a dense jungle had arisen on the spot where the snug homes and rich fields had been.

7 The King's Ankus

Kaa and Mowgli were bathing in the wise snake's favorite pool. They lay soaking in the cool water, watching the moon rise. Mowgli said to Kaa, "The man pack, at this hour, would lay down on hard pieces of wood. Shutting out the clean winds, they would pull dirty cloths over their heads. Then before long, they would begin to make evil songs through their noses. It is better in the jungle."

"So the jungle gives you all that you wish, Little Brother?" Kaa asked.

"I have the jungle," said Mowgli. "What more could there be between sunrise and sunset?"

Kaa said, "Three or four moons ago, I hunted in the Cold Lairs. There was a white cobra there who is the keeper of many things—*dead* things. He said a man would give the hot breath under his ribs just for the sight of them."

"We will go there to look then," said Mowgli,

"for I cannot forget that I was once a man."

Kaa and Mowgli set off for the Cold Lairs. This night they were empty and silent, for the Monkey-People were in the jungle. Kaa went down a ruined staircase in the queen's pavilion. Then he led Mowgli a great distance along an underground passage that finally opened into a vault.

"A well-hidden place," said Mowgli. "And now, what do we see?"

"*Am I nothing?*" The voice came from the middle of the vault. Mowgli turned and saw a cobra nearly eight feet long! Years of darkness had bleached him to an ivory white.

"Good hunting!" said Mowgli, whose manners never left him.

"What news of the city?" the cobra asked. "What of the great, walled city above our heads?"

"The jungle is above us," said Mowgli.

The cobra turned to Kaa. "Who is this man who is not afraid? How is it that he speaks our language with a man's lips?"

The boy spoke for himself. "Mowgli is what they call me. I am of the jungle. Now tell me, Father of Cobras, who are you?"

The cobra said, "I am the keeper of the king's

treasure. I teach death to those who come to steal."

Confused, Mowgli looked around and said, "But I see nothing here to take away."

"By the gods of the sun and moon!" cried the cobra. "Before your eyes close, I will let you see. You will look at what no man has seen before!"

Mowgli stared harder into the dim light of the dark vault. The floor was buried some five or six feet deep in silver and gold. There were golden candlesticks hung with emeralds. There were silver heads of forgotten gods with eyes of jewels. There were piles of swords, helmets, rings, bracelets, cups, and more—all decorated with silver and gold, rubies, diamonds, and jade.

Only one thing interested Mowgli, however. This was a two-foot *ankus*, or elephant goad. It was made of steel and ivory and decorated with jade, emeralds, rubies, and gold.

Mowgli said to the cobra, "Will you give me this if I will bring you frogs to eat?"

The cobra said, "Look by your foot!"

Mowgli picked up a man's skull.

The cobra said, "Behold a man who came here to take away the treasure."

Mowgli said, "If you will give me the ankus, it is good hunting. If not, it is good hunting also. I do not fight with you."

"No man who ever entered here has left," the cobra said. "I am the keeper of the city's treasure!"

Then Kaa cried, "*White worm!* There *is* no city! And what is this talk of killing?"

"If there is no city, there is still treasure," the cobra answered. "There is room for sport here. Watch me make the boy run."

Mowgli threw the ankus at the great cobra's hood, pinning him to the floor.

"*Kill!*" cried Kaa.

"No," Mowgli said. "I will never kill again—except for food. But look, Kaa!" Mowgli had forced the cobra's mouth open. Now Kaa could see that his fangs were black, dried up from age.

"I am shamed. Kill me!" hissed the cobra.

"There has been too much talk of killing," Mowgli said. "But I will take the ankus because I fought and beat you."

"You will not have it long, jungle man," the cobra warned. "My strength may be dried up, but the ankus will do its work. It is Death! I tell you, it is *Death*!"

Mowgli and Kaa were glad to leave the vault and return to the light of day. Mowgli quickly went to show the ankus to Bagheera.

"What do men use this ankus for?" Mowgli asked his friend.

Bagheera said, "It was made to poke at the heads of elephants, to make them obey. Since men have neither teeth nor claws, they create things like this—and worse."

Mowgli was disgusted. "It is always *blood* with this man pack. I will use this thing no more. Look!"

He threw the ankus 50 yards away, deep into the trees. Then he and Bagheera went to sleep.

That night Mowgli dreamed of the beautful object he had thrown away. When he woke to look for it, the ankus was gone.

"A man has taken it," Mowgli said to Bagheera. "Look—here is his trail."

They followed the trail most of the night. Soon it was clear that one man had been followed by a smaller man. Then, near a pile of broken rocks, lay a villager with an arrow in his back. The ankus was nowhere to be seen, and the smaller man's trail went on alone.

Mowgli and Bagheera followed the new trail to the ashes of a campfire. There lay the body of the smaller man, dead. The ankus was gone.

Mowgli stooped over the ashes. "*Four* men wearing shoes took the ankus," he said.

For another hour, they followed the trail. The day was clear and hot now. Before long they found another man lying in the bushes, dead. Around him was a circle of spilled flour.

"The cobra was right," said Mowgli. "This ankus is Death himself."

Half a mile farther, they found a smoking campfire. At its center, an iron plate held a burned cake of bread. Three men lay dead around it. Close to the fire, blazing in the sunshine, lay the ankus.

Mowgli tasted a piece of the bread and spat it out. "*Poison!*" he cried. "The man in the bushes must have put it in the bread for these three."

Mowgli picked up the ankus. "This goes back to the cobra," he said. "I have no love for men— but I would not have six of them die in one night!"

Two nights later, the cobra was sadly resting in the darkness of the vault. Then suddenly, the ankus flew in front of him and clashed on the floor of golden coins.

"Father of Cobras," said Mowgli. "Find a young cobra to help guard your treasure. No other man must come out of here alive."

"Aha!" said the cobra. "So the ankus returns, then. Why are *you* still alive?"

"I do not know," said Mowgli. "But let the ankus out no more."

8 Red Dog

When Mowgli was about 15 years old, Mother and Father Wolf died. Mowgli cried the Death Song over them. Baloo had grown old and stiff. Even Bagheera was slower at the kill. Akela walked as if made from wood, and Mowgli killed for him.

A young wolf named Phao had become leader of the wolf pack. For memory's sake, Mowgli came to the Council Rock, but he stayed by himself, or with his four wolf brothers. One night when he was hunting with them, they heard a terrible cry. Mowgli's hand flew to his knife.

"It must be a great killing!" cried Gray Brother.

They hurried to the Council Rock. There they found the pack listening and waiting. In a few minutes they heard tired feet on the rocks. Then a wolf flung himself into the circle, gasping. His sides were streaked with blood, his right forepaw useless.

"Good hunting!" said Phao. "Who are you?"

"Good hunting," replied the wolf. "I am an Outlier." Mowgli knew that an Outlier is a wolf who lives outside of any pack, taking care of his mate and cubs away from all others.

"What moves?" said Phao.

"The Red Dog of the Dekkan," the Outlier replied. "They came from the south, saying the Dekkan was empty of game. Now they come this way, killing all they meet. When this moon was new, there were four to me—my mate and three cubs. At dawn I found them stiff on the grass. I went after the Red Dog and found them."

"How many?" said Mowgli.

"I do not know. Three of them will kill no more, but at last they drove me like a deer. In a few days, a little strength will come back to me. Then I will fight them to pay my blood debt. But you, O wolves, you should go north until the Red Dog is gone."

"Hear the Outlier!" cried Mowgli, with a laugh. "We must go north and eat lizards and rats until the Red Dog is gone? No! This is good hunting! For the pack—for the lair and for the little cubs in the cave—we must fight!"

The pack answered with a chorus of deep crashing barks, "We *fight*!"

"Make ready for battle," cried Mowgli. "I go ahead to count the pack."

Wild with excitement, Mowgli ran off into the darkness. He hardly looked where he set his feet, and so tripped over the old snake Kaa, who was watching a deer path.

"*Kssha!*" said Kaa angrily. "Your noise will undo a night's hunting."

"Please forgive me. It was my fault," admitted Mowgli. "I was looking for you, Flathead. There is none like you in the jungle, O wise, strong, and most beautiful Kaa."

"Now where does this trail lead?" Kaa asked in a gentler voice.

Mowgli told Kaa of the Red Dog.

"Remember that this is the pack that cast you out," Kaa said. "Let the wolf fight the dog."

"It is true that I am a man," said Mowgli. "But this night it is in my stomach that I am also a wolf."

Kaa asked, "What do you plan to do when the Red Dog comes?"

"Make them swim the Wainganga!" Mowgli said. "I thought to meet them with my knife in the shallow water, the pack behind me. Have you a better plan, Kaa?"

For a long hour, Kaa lay wihout moving. He thought of all he had seen and known since he came from the egg. At last he said, "We will go to the river, and I will show you what can be done against the Red Dog."

Mowgli held onto Kaa as the great snake swam through the rapids. Soon they came to a gorge of marble rocks that were 80 to 100 feet high. On both sides, the gorge seemed to be hung with shining black curtains. These were the sleeping bodies of millions of the Little People—the busy, furious, wild black bees of India. On a sandbar below the cliffs lay the skeletons of many deer and buffalo.

"The Little People's kill," said Kaa. "*Think*, Mowgli! Hathi and the tiger himself turn aside for the Red Dog. And the Red Dog turn aside for no one. And yet for whom do the Little People turn aside? Who is the master of the jungle?"

"These," whispered Mowgli. "Come. This is a place of death. Let us go."

"They do not wake till dawn," said Kaa. "Now, many rains ago a buck came running here, a pack on his trail. Blinded with fear, he leaped over the gorge. The pack followed, but many were dead before they reached the water. Only the buck lived.

How do you think that happened?"

"*How?*" Mowgli demanded.

"Because he came *first*—before the Little People were aware," said Kaa.

"The buck lived," Mowgli said slowly.

"At least he did not die then," said Kaa. "Of course, he had no fat old Flathead waiting to pull him through the rapids."

Mowgli whispered, "Why, we will pull the very whiskers of death. Oh, Kaa—you are the wisest in all the jungle!"

Kaa said, "For your sake only I will carry word

to the pack. Soon they will know where to look for the Red Dog. I leave you here."

Mowgli gathered a small bundle of garlic, which he knew the Little People disliked. Then he went to find the Outlier's trail.

The trail, marked with blood, ran under a forest of trees that grew thinner and thinner as it neared the Bee Rocks. Mowgli waited in a tree, sharpening his knife on the bottom of his foot.

Before midday, the Red Dog came, following the trail. "Good Hunting!" called Mowgli. "Who gives you leave to hunt here?"

The pack slowed to a stop beneath Mowgli's tree. There were 200 of them, tall red dogs with heavy shoulders. One dog showed his teeth and said, "*All* jungles are our jungles."

"Dog, red dog!" Mowgli teased. "Go back to the Dekkan and eat lizards!"

The pack lept and snapped at him. Mowgli told them exactly what he thought of their manners, their customs, their mates, and their puppies. The Red Dog began to growl and then to yell with rage.

At last their leader made a great leap toward Mowgli. Mowgli grabbed him by the neck. While the branch under him shook, Mowgli pulled him up, inch by inch. Then he reached for his knife and cut off the dog's red, bushy tail, letting the dog fall back to the ground. That was all he needed. Now the Red Dog pack was furious. They would not leave Mowgli until they had killed him.

Mowgli waited in the tree until the sun had almost set. Then he lept from tree to tree, toward the Bee Rocks. The Red Dog followed hungrily. Then Mowgli came to the last tree. From here to the Bee Rocks was a stretch of open ground. After rubbing himself all over with garlic, Mowgli threw the leader's tail at the pack. Then he jumped to the ground and ran like the wind toward the Bee Rocks, the dogs howling behind him.

As he reached the edge of the gorge, Mowgli heard a roar like the sea in a cave. The air behind him grew black! Leaping outward with all his strength, he landed feet first in the water. There was not a sting on his body.

Then Mowgli could feel Kaa's strong body carrying him along. Red Dogs were falling through the air like black lumps. Every one of them was covered with hundreds of stinging bees!

Nearly half of the dog pack had seen what the others had rushed into. Now they turned aside and entered the river farther down. Seeing this, Mowgli dove off Kaa's back and found a couple of the swimming dogs with his knife.

The current soon swept them along to a sandy bank where the wolf pack waited.

"I leave you here," said Kaa to Mowgli. "I do not help wolves."

The Red Dogs crawled out of the water to meet the wolves. They were tired from swimming—their coats were wet and heavy.

It was a hard fight, loud with yells and snaps and cries. Mowgli's knife came and went. His wolf brothers fought by his side. At last the Red Dog grew weaker. It was the Outlier himself who killed the Red Dog leader.

"The blood debt is paid, Outlier," said Mowgli.

"Yes, their leader hunts no more," said Gray Brother, "but Akela is silent, too."

Seeing the Red Dogs retreating from the battle, Mowgli shouted, "They have killed Akela! Do not let a single dog go!"

He ran to Akela's side. The old wolf said, "It is good hunting. I would die by you, man-cub."

"No, no, I am a *wolf*!" Mowgli insisted. "It is no will of mine that I am also a man."

"Today you have saved the pack," said Akela. "All debts are paid. Go now to your own people. Hurry—before you are driven."

"Who will drive me?" said Mowgli.

"Mowgli will drive Mowgli," Akela sighed.

Then Akela sang the Death Song and fell silent upon his last kill.

Twenty-one of the wolves lay dead by the river. And every living wolf carried a terrible wound. But of all the pack of 200 Red Dogs, not one was left alive to carry the news to the Dekkan.

9 The Spring Running

It was the second year after the great fight with the Red Dog. Mowgli was nearly 17 years old now, and things had changed. The Jungle-People had once respected him for his wits. Now they respected him for his strength. But the look in his eyes was always gentle.

It was spring in the jungle, the Time of New Talk. All the smells were new and wonderful. Day and night you could hear a deep hum—not the hum of bees or falling water or the wind in the treetops. It was the purring of the warm, happy world.

One day Bagheera, too, was purring and singing to himself.

"Why are you singing?" asked Mowgli. "There is no game here."

Bagheera laughed. "Little Brother, are both your ears stopped? This is no killing song. It is the song I will sing to my mate."

Mowgli frowned and said, "I had forgotten it was the Time of New Talk. You and the others always run away and leave me alone. Remember last spring? When I sent for Hathi?"

"It took him only two days to come to you," Bagheera said patiently.

"He should have come on the night I sent for him. *I* am master of the jungle!" Mowgli cried out boastfully.

For some reason, Mowgli was in a bad temper. He had always loved the turn of the seasons. Spring was the season he made his long runs, just for the joy of it. Between twilight and the morning star, Mowgli would often dash 30, 40, or 50 miles. Then he would come back, panting and laughing, wearing strange flowers around his neck.

But this spring something was wrong. Mowgli felt hot and cold at the same time—and *angry* with something he could not see. Tonight, he decided, he would make a run to the distant marshes of the north and back again.

When he called to his four wolf brothers, however, not one of them answered. A couple of young wolves ran by, looking for a place to fight. Mowgli had never interfered in a spring fight before. Now he did, just to keep them quiet. He caught both wolves by the throat. But they knocked him down without a word and started to fight again.

In a flash, Mowgli was on his feet, his knife drawn. But suddenly the strength seemed to go out of his body. "I must have eaten poison," he said to himself. "Soon I may die!" He felt a sharp sadness he had never known before.

Still, he made his run to the marshes. As he ran through the jungle, he found himself singing out in pure joy. All the creatures of the jungle seemed to be singing or fighting around him.

Yet when Mowgli reached the marshes, the strange unhappiness came over him again—ten times worse than before!

Seeing Mysa the Wild Buffalo at the marshes, Mowgli could not resist teasing him. Sneaking up behind him, Mowgli pricked him with the point of his knife. The great bull broke out of the mud like a volcano exploding.

Mowgli laughed. "Now you can say that Mowgli, the hairless wolf, has herded you."

"Wolf? *You?*" snorted Mysa angrily. "All the jungle knows you once herded tame cattle. You are just like those men in the village nearby."

"What village, Mysa?" Mowgli asked.

"To the north," said Mysa. "Go tell *them* the kind of foolish jokes you play!"

"I will see this village," said Mowgli. He ran on toward the end of the marsh, where he saw a light. The glow of the Red Flower drew him on as if it were fresh game.

As Mowgli came near to the village, dogs began to bark. The door of a hut opened, and a woman looked out into the darkness. Then a child cried, and the woman whispered, "Sleep! It was only a jackal that woke the dogs."

Mowgli began to shake. He knew that voice. In man-talk he cried out, "Messua!"

"Who calls?" the woman answered in a shaking voice. "If it is you—what name did I give you?"

"Nathoo!" said Mowgli as he stepped forward into the light.

"My son!" she cried. "But I see you are no longer my boy. You are a god of the woods!"

At 17, Mowgli was indeed strong and tall and beautiful. His long black hair fell over his shoulders. His knife swung at his neck.

As he stepped into the hut, Messua said, "Are you *really* the one I called Nathoo?"

"I am," said Mowgli, with a soft smile. "I did not know you were here."

"A new English law allowed us to return to the village," explained Messua. "But when we went back, the village was no more to be found."

"I remember that," said Mowgli. "But tell me, Mother—where is your man?"

"He is dead—a year ago."

"And he?" Mowgli pointed to the child.

"My son was born two rains ago. If you really are a god, you must give him the protection of the jungle—just as you blessed us that long ago night when we went to Khanhiwara."

Messua lifted up the child, who tried to reach Mowgli's knife. Gently, Mowgli pushed away the little fingers.

"What do I know of this thing called a *blessing*?" Mowgli cried. "I am not a god, and—O Mother, my heart is heavy in me." He shivered as he put the child down on the cot.

Then Messua gave Mowgli warm milk, which made him sleepy. He lay down on the floor and slept the rest of the night and the next day. When he woke, he was ready to finish his spring running. But now the baby wanted to sit in his arms again. Messua insisted on combing out Mowgli's long, blue-black hair and singing to him.

Then Mowgli heard Gray Brother whining outside the hut. Messua's jaw dropped in horror.

"Do not worry. Think of the night on the road to Khanhiwara," said Mowgli. "I see that even in the spring, the Jungle-People do not forget me. Mother, I must go now."

Messua threw her arms around Mowgli's neck. "Son or no son, come back again—for I love you," she said. "Look! The baby will miss you, too!"

The child was crying because the man with the

shiny knife was going away.

Mowgli's throat hurt. "I will, Mother," he said. "I will come back."

Then Mowgli and Gray Brother left, following a path away from the village. When a girl in white came down the path, Mowgli and Gray Brother disappeared into a field of tall crops. Thinking she had seen evil spirits, the girl screamed. Then she gave out a deep sigh. Mowgli watched her until she had hurried out of sight.

"Bagheera was right," Gray Brother said. "Man goes to man at last."

Mowgli said, "What do you say?"

"Man cast you out once," Gray Brother explained. "They sent Buldeo to kill you. But it was you, not I, who said they were evil. You, and not I, let the jungle into their village."

"I don't know what you are saying," Mowgli said.

"I say you are master of the jungle," Gray Brother went on. "Even though I forget a little in the spring, your trail is my trail. Your kill is my kill. And your death fight is my death fight. But what will you say to the jungle?"

"Tell them all to come around to the Council Rock tonight," Mowgli answered. "There I will tell them what is in my stomach."

Gray Brother ran to the Jungle-People, calling out, "The master of the jungle goes back to man! Come to the Council Rock!" In any other season, they would have come. But it was spring.

"We will return in the summer heat," they called out to Gray Brother. "Come! Run and sing with us!"

Only the four wolves, Baloo, and Kaa came to the Council Rock that night.

"So your trail ends here, manling?" Kaa asked.

Mowgli threw himself down, his face in his hands. "I would not go," he sobbed, "but I am pulled by both feet. How shall I leave these nights?"

Old Baloo said, "You must mark your own trail—make your lair with your own blood. But when there is need of foot or tooth or eye, remember that the jungle is yours at your call. It is no longer the man-cub that asks leave of his pack. It is the master of the jungle who changes his trail. Who shall question man and his ways?"

Mowgli said, "But when I was still just a cub, Bagheera bought my place in the pack with the dead bull—"

His words were cut short by a roar in the brush below. Bagheera stretched out a dripping paw.

"A bull lies dead in the bushes now—a bull in his second year. This is the bull that frees you, Little Brother." Then he bounded away, crying, "Good hunting on your new trail, master of the jungle! Remember that Bagheera loved you!"

And this is the last of the Mowgli stories.